Karen's Big Sister

Look for these
and other books about Karen
in the
Baby-sitters Little Sister series:

Little Sister

Karen's Big Sister
Ann M. Martin

Illustrations by Susan Tang

A
LITTLE APPLE
PAPERBACK

SCHOLASTIC INC.
New York Toronto London Auckland Sydney

No part of this publication may be reproduced in whole or in part, or stored in a retrieval system, or transmitted in any form or by any means, electronic, mechanical, photocopying, recording, or otherwise, without written permission of the publisher. For information regarding permission, write to Scholastic Inc., 555 Broadway, New York, NY 10012.

ISBN 0-590-26193-2

12 11 10 9 8 7 6 5 4 3 2 1   6 7 8 9/9 0 1/0

Printed in the U.S.A.   40

First Scholastic printing, January 1996

The author gratefully acknowledges
Stephanie Calmenson
for her help
with this book.

Karen's Big Sister

Snowy Saturday

*S*crape, *scrape, scrape.*

I knew that sound very well. It had been waking me up a lot lately. It was the sound of shovels scraping the sidewalk.

It was a Saturday morning in January. There had been one snowstorm after another ever since Christmas. I did not mind one bit. I love snow!

I was in my room at the big house. (I have two houses — a big house and a little house. I will tell you more about them later.) I popped out of bed and peered out the window. The snow was deep.

I got dressed as fast as I could. I wanted to build a snowman. Or a snow fort. I had to get busy!

Who am I? I am Karen Brewer. I am seven years old. I have blonde hair, blue eyes, and a bunch of freckles. Oh, yes. I wear glasses. I have two pairs. I wear my blue pair for reading. I wear my pink pair the rest of the time. (I wish I did not have to wear glasses in the snow. When they get wet, I cannot see through them.)

I put on my boots, ski jacket, hat, and mittens. Then I ran downstairs. (I did not stop for breakfast. I could not wait to get outside.)

"Hi, Daddy!" I said. "Hi, Elizabeth. Hi, Sam. Hi, Charlie!"

Everyone was outside shoveling snow. Elizabeth is my stepmother. Sam and Charlie are my big brothers. (Sam and Charlie are so old they go to high school.)

"Hi, Karen," said Daddy. "Do you want to help us shovel a path?"

"Sure," I replied.

Shoveling snow to make a path is a grown-up thing to do. I decided my snowman could wait. I ran to the garage to get my red shovel. It is smaller than the grown-ups' shovels, but it works very well.

I helped shovel the path for about three seconds. Then my brothers, David Michael and Andrew, came outside. (David Michael is seven, like me. Andrew is four going on five.)

"Do you want to build a snowman with us?" asked Andrew.

I looked at Daddy.

"Go have fun," he said.

We did have fun. First we made three small snowmen. Then my sisters, Kristy and Emily, ran outside. (Kristy is thirteen. Emily is two and a half.) We decided to make one great big snowman together. Next, we made a snowlady. We made arms

and faces for our snow family out of sticks and stones. (We had to dig the stones out from under piles of snow.)

"Karen! Andrew!" called Nannie. (Nannie is our stepgrandmother.) "There is a telephone call for you."

"It is probably Mommy," I said to Andrew. "Come on!"

We ran inside and talked to Mommy. She calls us sometimes just to say hello when we are living at the big house. When we are not at the big house, we are at the little house. Then Daddy calls from the big house to say hello.

This may sound confusing to you. But it is not confusing to Andrew and me. We have lived in two different houses for years. It is not hard once you get the hang of it. I will tell you how it works.

Living in Two Houses

First I will tell *why* I live in two houses. It started a long time ago. When I was little, I lived in one big house in Stoneybrook, Connecticut, with Mommy, Daddy, and Andrew. Then Mommy and Daddy started to fight a lot. They told Andrew and me they loved us very much. But as hard as they tried, they could not get along with each other anymore. So Mommy and Daddy got a divorce.

Mommy moved with my brother and me to a little house not too far away. Then she met a very nice man named Seth. Mommy and Seth got married. So Seth is my stepfather.

This is who lives at the little house: Mommy, Seth, Andrew, me, Midgie (Seth's dog), Rocky (Seth's cat), Emily Junior (my pet rat, who I named after my sister, Emily), and Bob (Andrew's hermit crab).

Daddy stayed at the big house after the divorce. (It is the house he grew up in.) Then he met Elizabeth. Daddy and Elizabeth got married and that is how Elizabeth became my stepmother. Elizabeth was married once before and has four children. You know who they are. They are Kristy, David Michael, Sam, and Charlie.

I told you about my sister, Emily Michelle. But I did not tell you yet that she was adopted from a faraway place called Vietnam.

And I did not tell you that Nannie is Elizabeth's mother. She came to live at the big house to help take care of Emily. But really she helps take care of everyone.

There are pets at the big house, too. They are Shannon (David Michael's big Bernese mountain dog puppy), Boo-Boo (Daddy's cranky old tabby cat), Crystal Light the Second (my goldfish), and Goldfishie (Andrew's you-know-what). Oh, yes. Emily Junior and Bob live at the big house whenever Andrew and I are there.

When are we there? My brother and I switch houses every month. (Once in a while we stay at one house or the other for two months in a row.)

Now I will tell you *how* we live in two houses. We have a special system. We have two of lots of different things. That way we do not have to carry so much back and forth. I even have a special name for Andrew and me. I call us Andrew Two-Two and Karen Two-Two. I thought up those names after my teacher read a book to our class. It was called *Jacob Two-Two Meets the Hooded Fang*.

We are two-twos because we have two houses and two families, two mommies and two daddies, two cats and two dogs. We each have two sets of toys, clothes, and books. I have two bicycles. Andrew has two tricycles. I have two stuffed cats. Goosie lives at the little house. Moosie lives at the big house. I have two pieces of Tickly, my special blanket. And I have two best friends. Nancy Dawes lives next door to the little house. Hannie Papadakis lives across the street and one house over from the big house. Nancy and Hannie and I are in the same second-grade class at Stoneybrook Academy. We call ourselves the Three Musketeers. That is because we like to do everything together.

So now you know all about living in two houses. It does not sound hard, does it?

A Very Surprising Announcement

On Monday morning, I rode the bus to school with Hannie. I was glad it was a short trip. I do not like sitting on the bus bundled up in winter clothes.

Nancy was already at her desk when we walked into our classroom. She and Hannie sit at the back of the room. I used to sit there with them. Then I got glasses and Ms. Colman moved me to the front of the room. She said I could see better there. She was right.

I did not get to visit with Nancy because

Ms. Colman arrived. I waved to Nancy and went to my seat. Ms. Colman hung up her coat, then said, "Hannie, it is your turn to take attendance today."

Boo. I wished it were my turn. But if it had to be someone else's turn, I was glad it was Hannie's.

Hannie took the attendance book. She looked at Nancy and me first and checked off our names. (The Three Musketeers stick together.)

I looked around to see who else was in class. Ricky Torres and Natalie Springer were there. They are the other glasses-wearers who sit in the front row with me. (Ricky is my pretend husband. We got married on the playground at recess one day.) Pamela Harding, Jannie Gilbert, and Leslie Morris were there. (Pamela is my best enemy. Jannie and Leslie are her friends.) Addie Sidney was there. (She was peeling Christmas stickers off her wheelchair tray and putting snowman stickers in their place. Addie loves stickers!) Bobby Gianelli

11

was there. (He used to be a bully sometimes. But he is not anymore.) Sara Ford
was there. Hank Reubens was there. Omar
Harris was there.

A few kids were out sick. Hannie finished
marking the book, then handed it to Ms.
Colman.

"Thank you, Hannie. Now I have an an-
nouncement to make," said Ms. Colman.

Yippee! I love Ms. Colman's Surprising
Announcements. They are usually about
very good things, such as trips and special
projects. I sat up tall and listened.

"I want to share some good news of
mine. The good news is that I am going to
have a baby," said Ms. Colman.

"A baby? All right!" I called out.

This was a *very* surprising announce-
ment. I was so excited, I almost fell off my
chair. Everyone started asking questions at
once.

"I appreciate your enthusiasm, class,"
said Ms. Colman. "But I would still like you

to use your indoor voices. And please raise your hands."

Natalie raised her hand and Ms. Colman called on her.

"Are you still going to be our teacher?" she asked. Natalie is a big worrier. I did not blame her for worrying now. I would hate to lose Ms. Colman. She is the most wonderful teacher. She always thinks up interesting projects for us. And she never gets angry or yells at anyone. Not even me.

"This is what will happen," replied Ms. Colman. "I will be in school for several more months. After I have the baby, I will take off two months. Then I will return to school and be your full-time teacher again."

Omar raised his hand.

"Who will be our teacher while you are gone?" he asked.

"Mrs. Hoffman will take over," replied Ms. Colman.

This was good news. Mrs. Hoffman had been our teacher once before. At first we did not like her. She had too many rules. For a while I even called her "Hatey Hoffman." But she turned out to be nice. Now she is our favorite substitute teacher.

I was going to miss Ms. Colman. But she was going to be away from us for a very good reason. She was going to have a baby.

A baby! Hooray.

The Mystery Package

"See you tomorrow," I said to Hannie when we hopped off the bus after school.

I walked up the street to the big house. Daddy was just coming out to get the mail.

"Hi, Daddy!" I said. "Guess what we found out at school today."

I told Daddy Ms. Colman's news.

"That is terrific!" replied Daddy. "I am very happy for Ms. Colman."

Daddy took the mail from the mailbox and started sorting through it. There was a lot. I saw magazines and letters. I saw a small package, too.

"What is that?" I asked.

"I do not know," replied Daddy. "It has my name on it. But I do not recognize the return address."

"Let's hurry up and open it," I said.

Ooh. More surprises!

No one else was at home. It was just Daddy and me. And the mystery package.

Daddy opened the package carefully. Inside was a small box with a letter on top. Daddy read it.

Then he said, "The letter is from a lawyer telling me that a distant cousin of mine has passed away. She was an elderly woman named Louisa. I met her only a couple of times. She was very nice. I am sorry she is gone. It seems she has left me a family heirloom."

"What is an heirloom?" I asked.

"It is something that is handed down through a family. When one person passes away, he or she leaves it to someone else," said Daddy. "Louisa has left me a valuable pin. It has been in my family for many years."

Daddy opened the box. Inside it was a beautiful pin sitting on a bed of cotton. It was gold with diamonds and pearls on it. Ooh.

"May I hold it?" I asked.

"Yes, you may," replied Daddy.

I held the pin. It was heavy. It felt important. I handed it back to Daddy.

That night at dinner, Daddy told everyone about Cousin Louisa.

"She left me this pin, which has been in my family for years," said Daddy, holding up the pin. "I would like to pass it along to another member of my family. I would like to give it to Kristy, my oldest daughter."

Did I hear right? Did Daddy say he was giving the pin to Kristy? Not to *me*?

The next thing I knew, Daddy walked to Kristy and handed her the pin. Kristy was so happy. Her face lit up. She even started

to cry a little. I felt like crying, too. That was because I was mad. I was mad at Daddy for not giving the pin to me.

"Thank you," said Kristy. "The pin is beautiful. And it means a lot to me. It means I am really part of your family."

Hmmph. She was already part of the family. Daddy did not have to give her a pin to tell her that. She would never wear it anyway. It was too fussy.

I did not look at Daddy for the rest of dinner. When we finished, I followed Kristy to her room.

"Will you let me borrow the pin sometimes?" I asked.

Kristy looked at the pin. Then she looked at me.

"I am sorry, Karen," she said. "But this pin is really valuable. It is real gold with diamonds and pearls. It has been in the family forever. I would like to let you borrow it. But it would be terrible if it got lost."

"I will not lose it," I said. "I promise."

"I cannot take any chances," replied Kristy. "The pin means too much to me."

Boo and bullfrogs! I stomped off to my room. I love Daddy. I love Kristy. But I was mad at both of them.

Hurt Feelings

I spent two days stewing about the pin. I talked to Daddy and Kristy only when I had to. Only to say things such as "Please pass the butter," and "Excuse me."

On Tuesday night instead of watching TV with my family, I went to my room. I drew a picture of the pin. I made my picture the same size as the real one. I thought about cutting out the picture and wearing it. But a piece of paper could never look like a real gold pin with diamonds and pearls. No way.

"How could they do what they did, Moosie?" I asked. "How could Daddy give the pin to Kristy instead of me? How could Kristy say no when all I asked was to borrow the pin?"

I held Moosie up to my ear. I thought he might have something helpful to say. But he did not.

By Wednesday night, I was tired of moping and stewing. I decided to ask Kristy one more time about the pin before I went to bed. I knocked on her door.

"Come in," she called.

I did not waste any time. I asked her my question right away.

"I came to ask again if I can borrow the pin," I said. "I know you said no before. But maybe you changed your mind."

"I am sorry, Karen. I did not change my mind," replied Kristy. "I think the pin is too valuable to take a chance with. And it means too much to me."

That made me mad all over again.

"You will never even wear it," I said. "It

is just going to be wasted sitting in your jewelry box."

"Some things have more than one purpose," replied Kristy. "I do not think Watson gave me the pin because he expected me to wear it. I think he gave me the pin because he wanted to show me in a very nice way that he considers me his daughter."

"That is not true," I replied. "I am his *real* daughter. You are only his stepdaughter."

Kristy stared at me for a moment. Then her eyes filled with tears. "Karen Brewer!" she finally said. "How can you say something like that? You hurt my feelings. After all this time, how can you still think that way? I thought we were close. I thought we were family. *Real* family. Real sisters."

I had not expected that from Kristy. At first I did not know what to say. Finally I said, "Well, you hurt my feelings, too. Real sisters lend each other things. I do not see why you will not lend me the pin."

"You know I lend you things all the

time," said Kristy. "I explained my reasons for not wanting to lend you this pin. It would be nice if you were more understanding about it."

"Well, I do not understand," I replied. "Not at all."

"Neither do I," said Kristy.

I walked out of Kristy's room in a huff and went to bed. It took me a long time to fall asleep.

Karen's Cool Idea

I felt better when I woke up on Thursday morning. I put on my gray leggings and a purple-and-pink-striped sweater.

"The pin would look awful with this outfit anyway," I said to Moosie.

I hurried downstairs to eat breakfast. Kristy did not even say good morning to me. I guess she was still upset from the night before. I was happy when it was time to leave for school. I did not feel like thinking about Kristy and the pin. I had something more important to think about — Ms. Colman's baby!

That was all Hannie and I talked about on the school bus. We tried to guess if the baby would be a boy or a girl. We wondered what Ms. Colman would name it. We wondered how much it would weigh.

"Maybe she will have twins," I said.

"Or triplets," said Hannie.

"If she has triplet girls, she could name them Karen, Hannie, and Nancy!" I said.

When we reached school, Ms. Colman was already at her desk. She asked Addie to take attendance. (I hoped it would be my turn again soon.)

While Addie was checking off names, I started thinking. A new baby called for a celebration. A big celebration. Then I got a very cool idea. I decided my classmates and I should have a baby shower for Ms. Colman. I could hardly wait to tell everyone.

I whispered to Ricky, "Meeting at recess. Pass it on."

Ricky whispered to Bobby. Bobby whispered to Audrey Green. Audrey whispered to Omar. Soon the whole class knew about the meeting.

When recess finally came, the kids formed a big circle around me. (I wish I had a cool idea every day. I love being the center of attention.)

"It is very exciting that our teacher is having a baby," I said. "So I have an idea. I think we should have a baby shower for Ms. Colman."

"I bet Ms. Colman would love that!" said Sara.

"We could buy cute things for the baby," said Jannie.

"Do we have to wait for the baby to get here to have the party?" asked Ricky.

"I do not want to wait," said Natalie.

Nobody did. We wanted to have the party as soon as possible. We decided it should be a surprise, too.

"We will need some help planning an important party like this one," said Hannie.

I said I would talk to Daddy and Eliza-

beth when I got home. They could call the other parents. Then everyone could work together planning the baby shower.

"I think we should have streamers and balloons for decorations," said Nancy.

"We will need party food, too," said Addie. "We should have healthy food for Ms. Colman."

"And candy for us," said Bobby.

We talked about presents for the baby and how to surprise Ms. Colman. This party was going to be fun!

One More Try

At dinner that night, I told everyone about the baby shower. They thought it was a terrific idea. Even Kristy. I was happy that she did not seem upset with me anymore.

My entire family knows Ms. Colman and her husband, Mr. Simmons. (Mr. Simmons is a gigundoly nice high school principal.) The Simmonses have been to the little house and I have been to their house. I was invited to their wedding, too. (I was co-flower girl. Ms. Colman's niece was the other flower girl.)

After dinner, Daddy, Elizabeth, and Nannie sat down with me to talk about the party.

"We would like to have streamers and balloons. And we want to have healthy food for Ms. Colman," I said.

"Those are excellent ideas," said Daddy.

"Would you like to have the party at school, or here?" asked Elizabeth.

"I think we should have it at school. It will be easier to surprise Ms. Colman that way," I replied.

"What about gifts?" asked Nannie. "Will you all chip in and buy one gift? Or will each of you give her something?"

"We would like Ms. Colman to have lots of presents to open. So we will each give her something," I replied.

"We should call the other parents before it gets too late," said Daddy.

Daddy and Elizabeth made their calls while Nannie put Emily to bed. We have two phone lines, so they could both make calls at the same time. There are eighteen kids in my class. That meant there were sixteen phone calls to make. (They did not have to call me. And they only had to make one call for Terri and Tammy Barkan, the twins.)

There was nothing left for me to do, so I looked for Kristy. She was standing in the doorway of Charlie's room talking about her plans for the weekend.

"Tomorrow night I am going to a slumber party at Mary Anne's. On Saturday my friends and I are going ice skating in the afternoon," she said.

"I can drive you to Mary Anne's tomorrow," said Charlie. "I am going to a movie then. And I may be going ice skating on Saturday. So I will see you."

"Great," said Kristy.

When they finished talking, Kristy went to her room. I followed her there. I noticed that the pin was on her dresser. I guess she wanted to keep it out so she could look at it.

"Hi, Kristy," I said.

"Hi, Karen. How are your plans for the party going?"

"Okay," I replied. "Daddy and Elizabeth are calling the other kids' parents right now. I think the party is going to be fun."

"Oh, I do, too," replied Kristy. "It is so nice that Ms. Colman and Mr. Simmons are having their first baby."

Kristy was being very friendly. So I decided the time was right. I wanted to ask her one more time if I could borrow the pin.

"Um, Kristy," I said. "I know I asked you two times already, but . . ."

"Do not even finish the question," said Kristy. "The answer is no for the third time. You may not borrow my pin."

So much for being friendly. Kristy would not even let me ask the question. And I did not like the way she said *my* pin.

I decided I better leave before we got into trouble again.

What to Do?

After dinner on Friday, Charlie drove Kristy to Mary Anne's house.

"Drive carefully," said Daddy. "It is snowing pretty heavily."

As soon as they left, I ran to Kristy's room. I knew Kristy had not worn the pin. And I did not think she had taken it with her. She would be too afraid of losing it. And I wanted to look at the pin.

The pin was not on the dresser anymore. I was sure it was in her jewelry box. But I looked in a few other places first. I knew

Kristy would not like my snooping around. But I was mad at her. So I did not care.

I opened a couple of drawers. I did not see anything very interesting. Mostly turtleneck sweaters and T-shirts.

I looked in her closet next. I saw sneakers, jeans, and a couple of baseball bats. (Kristy is the coach of a softball team called the Krushers.)

Oh, well. I had snooped enough. I went to the dresser and opened the jewelry box. Just as I thought, the pin was there.

I picked it up. I ran my fingers over the smooth diamonds and pearls. I turned the pin over in my hand a couple of times. I had forgotten how heavy it was. It was definitely an important pin.

When I walked out of Kristy's room the pin was in my hand. I went back to my room and I showed it to Moosie. After all, I had already told him about it.

"Here is the pin, Moosie," I said. "It is really beautiful, isn't it?"

It was time to have a little talk with my-

self. One part of me said, "Put it back." The other part said, "Keep it." If I was going to return the pin, I knew I should do it right away. What did I do?

I put the pin in my own jewelry box. It looked nice and cozy. So I left it there overnight.

In the morning, I thought about returning it once and for all. Then I thought about wearing it. One part of me said, "Return it." The other part said, "Wear it." "Return it." "Wear it." "Return it." "Wear it." What did I do?

I got dressed and fastened the pin inside my sweater.

A Snowy Day

It was still snowing when I went downstairs for breakfast. It had been snowing all night long. Sam was in the kitchen listening to the weather report on the radio.

"The snow is expected to stop by mid-morning," said the announcer. "We should have up to eight inches by then."

"Hooray!" I said.

I love snow. It is so pretty.

I poured myself a bowl of Krispy Krunchy cereal. I sat there munching it and watching the snow falling down. The sky was gray. The snow was white. I felt as if I were sitting in the middle of a powder puff.

As soon as I finished breakfast, I bundled up to go outside. I was about to walk out the door with David Michael when the phone rang. Charlie answered it.

"It is for you, Karen. It is Hannie," he said.

"Hi, Hannie," I said. "What's up?"

It was a short conversation. Hannie was inviting me to come over to play.

"See you later, everyone," I said.

I grabbed my sled from the garage. Then I hurried across the street and rang Hannie's bell.

"I am so excited," said Hannie. "I want to do everything. We have to go sledding and build a snowman and throw snowballs. Come upstairs while I finish getting dressed."

While I was in Hannie's room, I remembered I was wearing the pin. I wanted to

39

show it off to Hannie. I opened my coat and my sweater.

"Look at this," I said. "It is my new pin. It is very valuable. These are *real* diamonds and pearls."

"Wow," replied Hannie. "Where did you get it?"

I told Hannie that Daddy had given me the pin.

"It was in his family for years and years. He wanted me to have it," I said.

"That is a neat gift," replied Hannie.

I knew Hannie would be impressed. After we bundled up in hats and mittens and scarves, we went outside. It was the perfect snowy day.

We dragged our sleds across the yard and went sledding with the kids in the neighborhood. After a while, David Michael and Linny showed up. (Linny is Hannie's older brother. He is nine.)

"Where is Andrew?" I asked David Michael.

"His throat hurt, so he had to stay inside," replied David Michael.

When we got tired of sledding, we went back to the Papadakises' house to warm up.

"Come have some lunch," said Mr. Papadakis.

We had egg salad sandwiches and hot chocolate with marshmallows. Yum.

As soon as we finished eating, we were ready to go outside again. We built a snow fort in the yard. David Michael and Linny built one, too. Then we had a snowball fight between the forts. The snow was soft and powdery. Our snowballs fell apart before they could hit anyone.

We saw a couple of cleanup trucks driving down our street. Their snowplows left huge hills of snow.

"Let's go!" said Linny.

We climbed up the hills and slid down. Up and down. Up and down. Even with all my clothes on, I was getting wet.

"Brr. I am cold," I said.

"Me, too," replied Hannie. "Let's go inside."

We went up to Hannie's room and peeled off our wet clothes. When I got down to my sweater, something did not feel right. My sweater felt lighter than it had before. I looked inside. Uh-oh.

"My pin!" I cried. "My pin! It is gone!"

The Search

"We *must* find it!" I said.

"I know," replied Hannie. "You told me the pin is very valuable."

That is not all, I thought to myself. I started bundling up again to go outside. I was so nervous I was having trouble zipping up my zipper. While I was tugging on it I blurted out, "Kristy will kill me."

"Why should Kristy care about the pin?" asked Hannie. "It is your dad who will be upset."

"They will both be upset," I mumbled. "It is not my pin."

"Huh?" said Hannie.

"It is not my pin," I repeated. "It belongs to Kristy. Daddy gave it to her, not to me."

"Then how did you get it? Did Kristy lend it to you?" asked Hannie.

"No," I replied.

I told Hannie the whole story. I told her how I took the pin from Kristy's jewelry box without her permission.

"You mean you stole it from her?" asked Hannie.

"Well, I borrowed it," I replied. "I was going to give it back. I just wanted to wear it for awhile. That is all."

I did not give Hannie a chance to ask any more questions. I just headed for the door.

"Come on," I said. "We have to start looking right away."

As soon as we got outside, my heart did a flip-flop. The snow did not look pretty to me anymore. It looked scary.

"We will just have to retrace our steps," said Hannie.

"We started on our sleds," I said. "We went across the front yard and up the street that way."

We followed our path. But by the time I reached the street, I felt hopeless. We had been sledding all over the place. And once the snowplows drove by, nothing was the same anymore.

We looked every place we might have been. We tunneled through snow drifts. We took apart our snow fort, then our snowman.

"Wait! I feel something at the bottom of the snowman," said Hannie.

I raced to her. I started jumping up and down.

"Did you find it? Did you really find it?" I cried.

"No," replied Hannie. "It is only a rock."

Boo. Just then a truck came plowing down the street. Another truck was behind that one. One truck was for plowing. The

other truck was for carting away the snow banks. Workers were loading the snow into the back of the second truck.

"If the pin is in one of those piles, it will be gone forever," I said to Hannie.

"Maybe the pin is buried somewhere in my yard," Hannie replied. "We will find it in the spring when the snow melts."

"Maybe you are right," I said. "But somehow I doubt it. Anyway, I cannot wait till spring. Kristy is going to be home in a couple of hours. She is not going to wait until spring to get upset."

Oh, boy. I was in a really big mess this time.

When to Tell?

"Thanks for helping me look for the pin, Hannie," I said.

I waved good-bye to my friend and went home. Kristy had not returned from ice skating yet. That was a relief. I was not ready to tell her about the missing pin. (When would I be ready? I was not sure.)

The first thing I did was put on dry clothes. After I took off my wet ones, I looked through them again. I did not find the pin. Oh, well. I had looked for it as hard as I could.

Andrew and Emily were in the kitchen with Nannie, so I went downstairs. They were having hot apple cider and cinnamon toast.

"Come join us," said Nannie. "I want to talk to you about the baby shower. Have you thought of a gift you would like to give Ms. Colman?"

"I would like to make something for her myself. I want my gift to be extra special," I said.

"How about a crib blanket?" asked Nannie. "You could knit one."

"That is a good idea," I said. "Only I have not knitted anything in a very long time. I am not sure I remember how."

"I will help you," replied Nannie. "You can knit small squares and sew them together. It is not very hard."

"All right!" I said. "Then I will have a personally designed, one-of-a-kind gift for my favorite teacher."

I finished my cider and went upstairs to draw a picture of the blanket I wanted to make. I decided to make it light pink, blue, and yellow. That would be pretty.

Kristy came home when it was almost time for dinner. I heard her go into her room. I waited a minute or two. I did not hear any screams. So I knew she had not looked in her jewelry box yet.

I put down my crayons and walked to my door. I took one step out of my room. I was going to tell Kristy about the pin. But I changed my mind. I went back into my room and closed the door.

At dinner, Kristy seemed friendly. She asked about my day. I told her about it. (Except the part about losing the pin, of course.)

After dinner, my family went into the den. We read, then watched TV. Everyone was relaxing. I did not want to upset them. So I did not tell Kristy then either.

"Good night, everyone," said Kristy when our show was over. "I will see you in the morning."

This is it, I thought. I am sure she will

want to look at her pin now. Should I tell her before she opens her jewelry box? Or should I explain after she finds out it is gone?

I decided I would run in and explain as soon as I heard her screaming. I waited and waited. But I did not hear anythng.

Phew. I knew Kristy was never going to wear the pin. She might not even look at it for a long time. Maybe I do not have to tell her now at all, I thought. If she finds out a long time from now that it is missing, I could make up a story. I could tell her something else happened to her pin. Something I had no part of. Hmm.

Party Plans

I decided I did not want to make up a story about the pin. That would not be right. I needed to tell Kristy the truth. But Sunday did not seem like a good day. Or Monday. Or Tuesday.

Oh, well. Kristy seemed to have forgotten about the pin anyway. I was thinking about it less and less, too. My classmates and I were spending a lot of time thinking about Ms. Colman's baby shower. We were making new plans every day.

The kids in my class and the grown-ups

agreed that the refreshments should be homemade. Nannie volunteered to organize the menu.

We also agreed to hold the party at the end of January. (Ms. Colman was not leaving then. But we could not stand to wait any longer than that.)

We decided that everyone in class who could afford it would donate five dollars by the end of the week to the party fund. The money in the fund would pay for decorations, plates, cups, napkins, and things like that.

Guess who was going to the mall to shop for the party supplies? Me! And Hannie and Omar. We were going with Daddy, Mrs. Papadakis, and Mrs. Harris on Friday. I could hardly wait. I love shopping for party things.

On Wednesday, the kids in my class held a meeting at recess. Audrey made a list of the gifts each of us wanted to give Ms. Colman. That way we would be sure Ms.

Colman would not get two of the same thing.

Some of the kids were going to buy gifts. The store-bought gifts on the list were a music box; baby books; a silver rattle, knife, fork, and spoon; a baby pillow and pillowcases to go with it.

Other kids, like me, were going to make gifts. The homemade gifts on the list were a crib blanket (made by yours truly); a picture frame; a photograph album; and a crib mobile.

A few kids had not decided what to give yet.

"We need to figure out how we are going to surprise Ms. Colman," said Hannie.

The bell rang then. It was time to go inside.

"Meeting again tomorrow at recess," I said.

On Thursday we met again.

"This morning I thought of a way we can

surprise Ms. Colman," said Nancy. "We could ask one of the other teachers to make sure Ms. Colman has playground duty the day of the party. While she is outside with us, our parents could sneak into the room and set everything up."

"When we go back inside after recess, all we have to do is shout, 'Surprise!' " I said.

"Then it will be party time," added Omar.

Our class liked Nancy's idea. I promised to tell Daddy and Elizabeth about it. I was sure they would think it was a good idea, too.

Everything was falling into place. And the next day was Friday. Washington Mall, here I come!

The Truth

On Friday afternoon, we bought everything we needed for the party. We bought light blue cups, yellow napkins, pink plates, and assorted colors of plastic knives, forks, spoons, streamers, and balloons. (I was happy the colors matched the blanket I was making.)

I went to bed thinking about Ms. Colman's party and feeling happy. I woke up on Saturday morning thinking about Kristy's pin and feeling sad. A week had passed since I lost it.

Kristy had not even mentioned the pin. She did not seem to miss it one bit. I decided that proved something. It proved she did not care much about it.

Thinking she did not care made me feel a little better about losing the pin. I got dressed and went down to breakfast.

"Nannie, can you help me with my blanket this morning?" I asked.

"Of course," replied Nannie. "You need one more practice lesson with me. Then you are on your own. You are doing very well."

I had forgotten how much I like knitting. I like the clickety-clack of the needles. I like watching a ball of yarn turn into a square of blanket.

We worked together in the morning. Then, after lunch, I went to my room to work some more on my own. (I did not like knitting downstairs so much. I kept having to shoo Boo-Boo away from the yarn.)

Clickety-clack. Clickety-clack. Knock, knock.

Kristy was standing at my door.

"Hi, Karen," she said. "Do you know where my pin is?"

Uh-oh. I was so surprised, I dropped a whole row of stitches in my knitting.

"Your what?" I asked. That was a dopey thing to say. I knew perfectly well what Kristy was asking. Kristy looked at me suspiciously.

"My pin, Karen. I would like to know if you have seen my pin," she said.

"No, I have not seen your pin," I replied. "I do not know anything about your pin. Except that you would not let me borrow it."

"Are you sure?" asked Kristy.

"I am absolutely, one hundred percent, positively sure," I replied.

"I am not sure I believe you, Karen," said Kristy.

"Why don't you look in your jewelry box where you left it?" I asked.

"How did you know it was in my jewelry box? The last time you were in my room it was on the dresser," said Kristy.

"Well, who leaves an important pin on a dresser?" I asked. "You must have put it in your jewelry box."

"I did not put it in my jewelry box," said Kristy.

"Oh, yes you did!" I replied.

Uh-oh. I should not have said that.

"You *did* see my pin!" said Kristy. "Please tell me where it is. I will not be angry as long as you give it back."

"I cannot give it back," I said.

"Why not?" asked Kristy.

"Because I borrowed it and lost it."

"You what? You lost my pin? How could you?" shouted Kristy.

Then she started to cry. A lot. I felt so bad, I started to cry, too. Finally Kristy stopped crying long enough to speak.

"I am very, very angry at you!" she said.

She ran to her room and slammed the door.

Karen's Note

Clickety-clack. Clickety-clack. It was Sunday morning. I was in my room knitting fast and furiously.

I had tried to talk to Kristy at breakfast. But she would not answer me. Daddy asked what was going on between us.

"We are having a little disagreement," said Kristy.

She still had not told Daddy that I lost the pin. She said this was between the two of us. She did not want to be a baby tattle-tale. Thank goodness.

I wanted Kristy to know that I was sorry, but that I would not have lost her pin if she had let me borrow it in the first place.

I decided to write her a note. I put down my knitting and found paper and a gold marker. I wanted the note to be written in gold letters in memory of the pin. The note said:

KRISTY,
   I AM SORRY I LOST THE PIN. YOU SHOULD HAVE LET ME BORROW IT.
                    SINCERELY YOURS,
                        KAREN
   P.S. I AM ATTACHING THE PAPER PIN I MADE IN CASE YOU WANT TO WEAR IT. (SEE, I LET YOU BORROW MY THINGS.)

I put the note and the paper pin in an envelope. Then I looked for Emily. If I delivered the note myself, Kristy might not read it. But if Emily delivered it, Kristy would read it before she realized it was from me.

Emily was not in her room. She was not downstairs either.

"Where is Emily?" I asked Elizabeth.

"Nannie took her to play with Sari for a while," Elizabeth replied. (Sari is Hannie's little sister. She is Emily's age.)

Bullfrogs. I needed Emily to help me. Just then Shannon ran into the room. Perfect. Kristy would never turn Shannon away.

"Shannon, come!" I said.

Shannon stood where she was. She turned her head and looked at me. At least I had her attention.

"Okay, Shannon. If you will not come to me, I will come to you," I said.

I held the note out to Shannon. All she did was drool on it. I wiped off the note. I tried again. It was no use.

"Wait here," I said.

I ran upstairs and found a piece of blue yarn. I punched a hole in the envelope and put the yarn through it.

Then I ran downstairs again. I tied the yarn with the note attached to it to Shannon's collar. I led her upstairs to Kristy's room and knocked on her door.

"Who is it?" asked Kristy.

I did not answer. I just opened the door and pushed Shannon inside. She must have jumped on Kristy because I heard her groan.

I waited to hear the sound of my note being opened. Instead I heard footsteps. I started to run back to my room, but Kristy caught me.

"In case you had not noticed, I am not talking to you," said Kristy. "And I am not reading any notes from you either!"

Hmmph. How did she guess the note was from me? Oh, well. I went back to my room to knit some more squares.

Friends

It was bad enough when Kristy was not talking to me. But things grew even worse when she refused to be in the same room with me. As soon as I walked into a room, she walked out. Except at mealtime. Then she made sure she did not have to sit near me.

After awhile, I started getting angry back at her. If I walked into a room and saw Kristy, I walked back out. One time we did not notice we were in the living room together because Kristy was bending down to look at something when I walked in. We almost crashed into each other trying to get out at the same time. (I thought I saw Kristy laugh a little. But I am not sure.)

This went on for days. Finally, Kristy said, "It is time for us to stop acting silly. Only babies behave this way."

"Well, I did not start it," I said. "I tried to talk to you and I tried to send you a note."

"You did too start it," replied Kristy. "You took my pin. And you lost it."

"I already told you I was sorry," I said. "But if you had not been so selfish and greedy about the pin in the first place none of this would have happened."

"I have every right to say no when you ask to borrow something. And you have no right to go ahead and steal it from me," said Kristy. "Furthermore, it was mean of you to say I am only a stepdaughter." Kristy paused. "I mean, it was *really* mean. I was serious when I said you hurt my feelings, Karen." Kristy's chin quivered.

"Oh, Kristy," I replied. "I am sorry. I did not mean that. And I did not mean to hurt your feelings. I said that because I was mad. And jealous. I felt bad because Daddy gave the pin to you instead of me. And I felt bad that you would not lend it to me."

"Well, I am sorry I did not lend you the pin. Maybe I should have trusted you with it," said Kristy.

There. We had both said we were sorry.

"Friends?" I said.

"Friends," replied Kristy.

Goody. Now that we were friends again, I wanted to do something for Kristy since I had lost the pin. I even thought of a way to replace her jewelry (sort of).

The Gift

I went to my room. I thought for a long time. Then I called Mommy. I made sure Kristy would not be able to hear me talking on the phone. If she heard me, the surprise would be ruined. I dialed the number at the little house.

"Hello, Mommy?" I said.

I whispered the rest of my conversation. I did not tell Mommy the whole story. I just said I wanted to give something special to Kristy. I told her what it was. She said it was okay with her.

"Thank you," I replied. "I will come over later to get it."

When Charlie returned I asked if he would give me a ride to Mommy's house.

"No problem," he said. "We can go right now if you want."

We drove there in the Junk Bucket. (That is the name of Charlie's car.)

"I just have to get something in my room. I will be right back," I said.

Mommy was the only one home. (The only person that is. Our pets were home, too.) I kissed Mommy hello, then ran to my room. I opened my jewelry box and found what I wanted right away. I put it in my sweatshirt pocket, then ran downstairs again.

"Thank you, Mommy," I said.

Charlie drove us back to the big house. We arrived just in time for dinner.

"Where did you two go?" asked Daddy.

"Charlie drove me to the little house. I wanted to get something," I replied.

As soon as dinner was over I followed

Kristy to her room with my gift.

"Um, there is something I would like to give you," I said. "It is a present."

"Really?" replied Kristy. "What is it?"

"Open the box and see."

Kristy opened the box. Inside was a bracelet. It was not an expensive bracelet. It was only costume jewelry. But it had once belonged to Mommy's great-aunt. Then Mommy gave it to me. Now I was giving it to Kristy. I thought this would end my problems with Kristy.

I was wrong.

"Thank you," said Kristy. "But I must tell you that I cannot accept this."

"Why not?" I asked.

"It belongs to your mother's side of the family," said Kristy. "This gift cannot replace the one Watson gave me. When he gave me that pin he was telling me that I was really and truly part of *his* family."

"Fine," I said. "I will take the bracelet

back. And I will not be giving you any other gifts very soon!"

This time I was the one who was angry. This time I was the one who was hurt. I stormed out of Kristy's room.

Making Up

I went straight to my room to get my knitting. Knitting made me feel better when I was angry. *Clickety-clack.* I was glad Nannie had given me extra yarn. If I kept knitting this way, the crib blanket was going to be a lot bigger than I had planned.

I was knitting in the den a few days later when Kristy walked in.

"Those squares look very pretty," she said.

I did not say thank you. I did not say anything. Maybe Kristy was not angry at *me*, but I was still angry at *her*.

I stood up and walked out of the room with my nose in the air. I will show you, I thought. But when I reached the door, I felt something tugging me back. My yarn was caught under the chair where I had been sitting. Oops.

"Here, let me get that," said Kristy, giggling. She thought this was very funny. I did not.

As soon as my yarn was untangled, I walked out again.

That night we had spaghetti for dinner. I did not want to sit near Kristy. But there were no other seats when I got to the table. I sat down with my knitting in my lap.

"How is it going?" asked Kristy.

I did not answer. I took a forkful of spaghetti and twirled it around on my spoon. Guess what I was thinking. I was thinking that being angry all the time was not so easy. For a minute I could not even remember what I was angry about. Oh, yes. Kristy did not accept the gift I gave her. I guess that was because she still felt bad about my losing her pin. Well, I still felt bad about it, too. I tried to make up for it with the bracelet. But that did not work. There was no way I could make up for losing the pin except by finding it. And that was not going to happen.

Even if I happened to find the pin someday, it would not take away the fact that I had borrowed it without permission in the first place.

I sighed. I was tired of not talking to Kristy. I was tired of being angry. After dinner I followed Kristy to her room one more time. I stood in Kristy's doorway and said, "I am really sorry I borrowed the pin when you told me not to. And I am really sorry I lost it."

"I know you are sorry, Karen," she replied. "You tried your best to make up for losing the pin by giving me the bracelet. But there is no making up for what you did. I appreciate your trying, though. And I forgive you."

"Do you really forgive me?" I asked. I needed to hear it one more time.

"Yes, I really and truly forgive you. You know, someday we will forget all this terrible fighting. We will be just the way we were before the whole thing started."

"I am glad," I replied. There was one thing left to do. "Um, Kristy. Will you come with me to tell Daddy about the pin? I am a little afraid to tell him myself," I said.

"Sure," replied Kristy.

I told Daddy the whole story. He was sorry I had been so upset about not getting the pin. But he was angry at me for taking it from Kristy.

"Taking the pin was not right," said Daddy. "But I am not going to punish you. I see that you and Kristy have worked this out on your own. I think maybe it has even brought the two of you closer together. And that is worth more than any piece of jewelry."

That was it. The fighting was over. There were no secrets from Daddy. I felt a whole lot better.

Getting Ready

Kristy and I had been friends again for ten whole days. That made me happy. I was also happy because there was only one more day until Ms. Colman's baby shower.

After school on Thursday, I hopped into the car with Daddy. We drove to each of my classmates' houses to pick up Ms. Colman's gifts and the food for the party. (We had volunteered to bring the food to school because many of the parents could not come to the party.)

The packages were all beautifully wrapped with paper that was decorated with everything from rocking horses to rattles. They were tied up with ribbons and bows.

The food looked and smelled delicious. (I got a sample brownie from Mrs. Harris. Yum.)

One gift was not quite ready. Mine!

"Will you help me finish the blanket now, Nannie?" I asked when Daddy and I returned home.

"Of course," replied Nannie.

I needed to sew together two more rows of squares. Nannie and I worked at the same time on opposite ends of the blanket. (The blanket did turn out to be bigger than I had planned. That was because I knitted so much while Kristy and I were fighting.)

Finally all the squares were sewn together. Nannie blocked the blanket for me. (She sprinkled it with water and ironed it lightly. That made it smooth and flat.)

"I cannot believe I made that!" I cried when it was ready.

My blanket was beautiful. I ran around showing it to everyone in my family. I even asked Daddy to take a picture of it for me to bring to the little house.

It was time to wrap my gift. I neatly folded my blanket and put it in a shiny white box with pink tissue paper. I tied on lots of colored ribbons. Kristy helped me make the ribbons curly.

"Ta-daa!" I said.

"You are all set for the party," said Kristy. "You should be very proud."

"Wait!" I cried. "The kids in my class forgot something. We forgot to make a card for Ms. Colman."

"That is no problem," said Kristy. "You are good at making cards."

She was right. I make special cards for all occasions. I got out my supplies — paper, markers, scissors, glitter, and glue. I folded a sheet of paper in half and drew a picture of my blanket on the front. I added a border of baby bottles and rattles. Inside I wrote: Good Luck, Ms. Colman!

The only thing left to do was to ask everyone to sign the card at school without Ms. Colman catching us.

I showed the card to Hannie on the school bus the next morning.

"That was a good idea," she said.

Hannie and a few other kids signed the card on the way to school. When we reached our class, Nancy and some more kids signed it fast before Ms. Colman arrived. Then we passed it under our desks for the rest of the kids to sign.

By recess, the card was ready. I hid it in my desk. (I had told Daddy where the card would be so he could put it with the gifts.)

On our way to lunch I turned and looked at our classroom. In one more hour it was going to be all dressed up.

At recess, we made believe we were choosing sides for a game. But really we were whispering about the party.

"Do you think our surprise will work?" asked Hannie.

"Do you think the room will be set up by the time we get back?" asked Omar.

We would know in just a few minutes.

Surprise!

Recess was over. The classes on the playground were lining up to go inside. It was party time.

Ms. Colman still had no idea what would be waiting for her when she entered the room. She led us into the building and down the hall. She opened the door and . . .

"Surprise!" we shouted.

"Oh, my!" said Ms. Colman. She was so surprised, she could not move. I took her by the hand and led her inside. The rest of the class rushed in behind us.

The room looked great. Daddy, Mrs. Papadakis, Mrs. Harris, and a few other parents were waiting for us. They had hung the streamers and balloons everywhere. They had moved four desks together in the center of the room. The desks were covered with a tablecloth and the food and plates and things were set out on them. Two more tables were pushed together and covered with another cloth. Those tables were piled high with presents.

"This is just wonderful," said Ms. Colman. "Thank you all very, very much."

"I think you are thanking us too soon," I said. "You have not even eaten any food, or opened any presents yet."

"I do not need a bite of food or a single gift to thank you for being so thoughtful," replied Ms. Colman. "But now that you mention it, that food smells awfully good."

We lined up and filled our plates with things to eat. There were pretzels and chips. There were brownies and cookies and a cake with pink and blue icing that said, "Best wishes, Ms. Colman."

When we had finished eating, Daddy said to Ms. Colman, "How about opening your presents now?"

The card was on top of the pile. A big smile spread across Ms. Colman's face when she opened it.

"I will keep this forever," she said. She was looking at me when she said it. I think she knew I had made the card.

Next, she started opening boxes. We had gotten her all the things on our list. When the class saw the blanket I made, they oohed and ahhed. I felt gigundoly proud.

One of the gifts Ms. Colman received was a tape of nursery rhymes set to music. We played it while we talked and laughed. Suddenly Ms. Colman smiled and said, "I know this song. My mother sang it to me when I was little." She began to sing along.

Up to the ceiling, down to the ground,
Backwards and forwards, round and round:
Dance, little baby, and mother shall sing,

With the merry gay choral, ding, ding,
ding-a-ding, ding.

I knew Ms. Colman was a wonderful teacher. I could tell from the way she sang the song that she was going to be a wonderful mommy, too.

Sisters Always

After school, I went to my room to drop off my jacket and my bookbag. I did not feel like having an after-school snack. I had eaten too much food at the party. But Nannie, Emily, and Andrew were waiting to hear how everything had turned out. I dropped off my things and ran to the kitchen.

"The party was great," I told them. "I wish you could have seen the look on Ms. Colman's face. She was so surprised.

Everyone loved my blanket. And, Nannie, they ate every last bite of the cookies you made."

"I am very glad they enjoyed them," said Nannie.

After dinner that night, I went to my room to get ready for the next day. There was not going to be a party, but it was another important day.

I looked at my calendar. I crossed off the party. It was January 31st, the last day of the month. The next day was February first. Andrew and I would be going back to the little house. We would live there for the month of February. We would return to the big house on March first.

It was time for me to pack a few things and say good-bye to Moosie, Crystal Light, and my big-house dolls.

I was picking out the books I wanted to take to the little house with me when Kristy knocked on my door.

"May I come in?" she asked.

"Sure," I replied.

She handed me a small gift-wrapped box.

"Thank you," I said.

"You are welcome. But you did not even open it yet," said Kristy.

"I do not have to open the present to thank you for being thoughtful," I said. (I said it just the way Ms. Colman had said it at the party.)

Then I ripped off the paper and opened the box. Inside was a gold-colored I.D. bracelet with writing on it. I picked it up and read it. It said *Sisters Always* in fancy script letters.

"It is beautiful!" I cried. "Thank you for real, Kristy."

"You are welcome for real."

Kristy pushed up the sleeve of her shirt. She was wearing an I.D. bracelet just like mine.

"This is the nicest present ever! Sisters always!" I said.

"Sisters always," repeated Kristy.

Kristy's gift was proof that she had truly forgiven me. Our fighting days had been over for awhile. We were Sisters Always. And we would be friends always, too.

About the Author

ANN M. MARTIN lives in New York City and loves animals, especially cats. She has a cat of her own, Gussie.

Other books by Ann M. Martin that you might enjoy are *Stage Fright*; *Me and Katie (the Pest)*; and the books in *The Baby-sitters Club* series.

Ann likes ice cream and *I Love Lucy*. And she has her own little sister, whose name is Jane.

Little Sister

Don't miss #70

KAREN'S GRANDAD

"Hi, Grandad," I said. "Want some company?"

"You know I always love to have your company, Karen," Grandad replied.

"I am going to ask Mommy if I can have my after-school snack in here. Do you want a snack, too?" I asked.

"No, thank you," replied Grandad. "I am not too hungry these days."

When I got back, Grandad was resting with his eyes closed. I looked around while I ate my snack.

Just then Grandad opened his eyes and smiled at me.

"You are back," he said. "How was school today? I would like to hear all about it."

LITTLE APPLE®

B·A·B·Y·SITTERS

Little Sister™
by Ann M. Martin, author of *The Baby-sitters Club®*

❑ MQ44300-3	#1	Karen's Witch	$2.95
❑ MQ44259-7	#2	Karen's Roller Skates	$2.95
❑ MQ44299-7	#3	Karen's Worst Day	$2.95
❑ MQ44264-3	#4	Karen's Kittycat Club	$2.95
❑ MQ44258-9	#5	Karen's School Picture	$2.95
❑ MQ44298-8	#6	Karen's Little Sister	$2.95
❑ MQ44257-0	#7	Karen's Birthday	$2.95
❑ MQ42670-2	#8	Karen's Haircut	$2.95
❑ MQ43652-X	#9	Karen's Sleepover	$2.95
❑ MQ43651-1	#10	Karen's Grandmothers	$2.95
❑ MQ43650-3	#11	Karen's Prize	$2.95
❑ MQ43649-X	#12	Karen's Ghost	$2.95
❑ MQ43648-1	#13	Karen's Surprise	$2.95
❑ MQ43646-5	#14	Karen's New Year	$2.95
❑ MQ43645-7	#15	Karen's in Love	$2.95
❑ MQ43644-9	#16	Karen's Goldfish	$2.95
❑ MQ43643-0	#17	Karen's Brothers	$2.95
❑ MQ43642-2	#18	Karen's Home Run	$2.95
❑ MQ43641-4	#19	Karen's Good-Bye	$2.95
❑ MQ44823-4	#20	Karen's Carnival	$2.95
❑ MQ44824-2	#21	Karen's New Teacher	$2.95
❑ MQ44833-1	#22	Karen's Little Witch	$2.95
❑ MQ44832-3	#23	Karen's Doll	$2.95
❑ MQ44859-5	#24	Karen's School Trip	$2.95
❑ MQ44831-5	#25	Karen's Pen Pal	$2.95
❑ MQ44830-7	#26	Karen's Ducklings	$2.75
❑ MQ44829-3	#27	Karen's Big Joke	$2.95
❑ MQ44828-5	#28	Karen's Tea Party	$2.95
❑ MQ44825-0	#29	Karen's Cartwheel	$2.75
❑ MQ45645-8	#30	Karen's Kittens	$2.95
❑ MQ45646-6	#31	Karen's Bully	$2.95
❑ MQ45647-4	#32	Karen's Pumpkin Patch	$2.95
❑ MQ45648-2	#33	Karen's Secret	$2.95
❑ MQ45650-4	#34	Karen's Snow Day	$2.95
❑ MQ45652-0	#35	Karen's Doll Hospital	$2.95
❑ MQ45651-2	#36	Karen's New Friend	$2.95
❑ MQ45653-9	#37	Karen's Tuba	$2.95
❑ MQ45655-5	#38	Karen's Big Lie	$2.95
❑ MQ45654-7	#39	Karen's Wedding	$2.95
❑ MQ47040-X	#40	Karen's Newspaper	$2.95

More Titles... ➡

The Baby-sitters Little Sister titles continued...

Available wherever you buy books, or use this order form.

- -

Scholastic Inc., P.O. Box 7502, 2931 E. McCarty Street, Jefferson City, MO 65102

Please send me the books I have checked above. I am enclosing $_____
(please add $2.00 to cover shipping and handling). Send check or money order - no cash or C.O.D.s please.

Name_____ Birthdate_____

Address _____

City_____ State/Zip _____

Please allow four to six weeks for delivery. Offer good in U.S.A. only. Sorry, mail orders are not available to residents to Canada. Prices subject to change.

Now THE BABY-SITTERS CLUB®

★ is a Video Club too! ★

LITTLE  APPLE®

*T*here are fun times ahead with kids just like you in Little Apple books! Once you take a bite out of a Little Apple—you'll want to read more!

Reading Excitement for Kids with BIG Appetites!